Some Homosexuals Will Go to Heaven!

Brenda A. Dudley

Some Homosexuals Will Go to Heaven!

Copyright © 2022 by Brenda A. Dudley.

Paperback ISBN: 978-1-63812-339-2
Ebook ISBN: 978-1-63812-338-5

All rights reserved. No part in this book may be produced and transmitted in any form or by any means, electronic, or mechanical, including photocopying, recording, or by any information storage and retrieval system, without permission in writing from the copyright owner.

The views expressed in this work are solely those of the author and do not necessarily reflect the views of the publisher hereby disclaims any responsibility for them.

Published by Pen Culture Solutions   07/10/2022

Pen Culture Solutions
1-888-727-7204 (USA)
1-800-950-458 (Australia)
support@penculturesolutions.com

This book is written with some intended grammatical errors and slang. I, the writer, took some advice from an old English teacher who suggested that I could.

Write your thoughts and questions here:

Love is the strongest force on the face of the earth.

Brenda A. Dudley

Write your thoughts and questions here:

To all people of all walks of life and all denominations.

People who judge others, people who are judged, young, old, rich, poor, in prison or out, sick or healthy, blind or deaf, and, for God's sake, politicians and the media ... This book does possess God's word.

To Peggy Lindsey, who helped me night after night, day after day, in editing, laughing, crying, and comforting me. Thank you, thank you, thank you.

To my loving daughter, Tammie Terrell Washington, who has been an unfailing inspiration in my life; my precious granddaughter, Mona'e Izzard; and grandtwins, Jayden and Jade Wilson, born many years later. I guess I had to wait for them.

To my family, who values forgiveness and love.

To all my extended family members who share in that love. To all my friends from near and far.

Much love to all of you!

You know that I'm not a liar. Many of you have witnessed some of these truths.

Write your thoughts and questions here:

In the beginning ...

You know what that means, don't you?

Brenda A. Dudley

Write your thoughts and questions here:

May God speak to your ears, eyes, or fingertips and, by all means, your heart!

There are 365 days in a year. People cry every day, every hour, every minute, and every second. Someone is crying *now*!

The Bible tells us that heaven is a place where there is no crying. If this is true, wouldn't you like to go there? The Bible also tells us that if we can believe, we can go to heaven. I decided to believe, in case this is true.

My child, accept thine own self. I love you as you are.

Brenda A. Dudley

Write your thoughts and questions here:

"That whosoever believeth shall not perish but have everlasting life."

Write your thoughts and questions here:

Some homosexuals will go to heaven.

My child, accept thine own self. I love you as you are.

Brenda A. Dudley

Write your thoughts and questions here:

It is so hard, so misunderstood, so unnoticeable, so condemned, so talked about, so preached about, and some more abouts … about gays or at-large homosexuals.

About homosexuals? Oh yeah, by the way or by the about, I'm one of them. No, I'm not out—I am about—and I'm about to tell you some truths about homosexuals going to heaven. I am one of them. Yes, I'm on my way to heaven. How do I know? Because the Bible says, "Whosoever believeth in Him should not perish but have everlasting life" (John 3:16). No one can ever take my belief from me. I believe! I don't need to prove my belief, for it's who I am, where I've been, and where I'm going. More importantly, I belong to the Lord. He died and rose for me, so yes, I believe. Therefore, heaven belongs to me also.

I am saved. Romans 10:9–10 says, "If thou shalt confess with thy mouth the Lord Jesus, and shalt believe in thine heart that God hath raised Him from the dead, thou shalt be saved. For with the heart man believeth unto righteousness; and with the mouth confession is made unto salvation."

That's how it all started. I heard about God loving me and Jesus dying for me. I believed, confessed, and got baptized. Baptized to have all my born-in-sin washed away and baptized to be born again in spirit. Yep, homosexuals going to heaven.

I'm not the only one who believes, who has been born anew and baptized. Many of us have been. One day I realized that I was gay. I had never heard the word *homosexual* or even *gay*— not that way, anyway—but when I found out, I *ran* to God to ask Him not to make me that way. I had always known I was different, but I'd never known how.

This is how I found out—really found out. I was incarcerated in Lexington, Kentucky. The institution housed male and female inmates, and we would mingle in a large courtyard. I saw a woman I had known as a child. We were around the same age. She was beautiful, and I was very attracted to her. Not because I missed Mommy or Daddy or because some man had hurt me so bad or because I was a sinner but just because—because I needed a woman's love. That's what the preacher had told me after my prayer to God.

This is what happened. Remember I said that I had *run* to God? Well, I did. On my unit we had a prayer room with candles on a table. I went there to talk to God. I got down on my knees and told God that I was afraid because I was different. I realized that I wanted a loving relationship with that woman, but how could that be, with men around?

I was afraid, and I begged God not to let me be that way. Someone said that I was gay—and I was, but I told God that I didn't want to be that way because I would be noticed. Men would look at me, point their fingers at me, and harm me. I wouldn't be like other people, or so I thought. Anyway, I was on my knees crying and praying, asking God to help me.

Can you imagine the fear and turmoil I felt? As I was sobbing, I got quiet. It was as if someone was trying to clear their throat, and I felt a presence a little above my head. I knew it was God because He spoke suddenly and quietly. He said, "My child, accept thine own self. I love you as you are." As I was still listening and trying to understand what He had just said, He spoke again: "My child, accept thine own self. I love you as you are." God said it twice, but I was still a bit confused, so He spoke a third time: "My child, accept thine own self. I love you as you are."

I was getting it—well, part of it anyway. I understood that He loved me, and I was immediately happy and relieved. All my fear was gone. It sure felt good to hear God say He loved me as I was, but He had also told me something else: to "accept thine own self." That part had me puzzled because I didn't know what the word *accept* meant. I couldn't look it up in the dictionary because I could barely read. Why? Because I had played hooky from school for most of my childhood. Nevertheless, God had spoken to me, and I needed to know what He meant. I didn't know who to ask or what to do. It felt good to know that God loved me, but what about accepting myself? How was I to do that, and what did it mean?

I was disturbed again but this time walking in a daze slowly. I felt that I didn't have a friend in the world—or should I say in prison. Yes, I was still in there. Then I thought about talking to the chaplain, but how could I explain it to him? He would think that I was crazy if I told him what had happened. Was I a chicken, or what? Well, maybe, but the chicken let the rooster out of the bag—much later, that is. But I figured the chaplain could help me, and he did, although it took a lot of me beating around the bush.

I said, "I need to talk to you."

"Okay, about what?" he asked.

"Well, I'm different."

"We're all different."

That didn't do it, I thought. "You know, like *different*."

He asked, "Different how?"

Feeling afraid again, I quickly asked, "What does the word *accept* mean?"

"Well, what do you mean?"

"I don't know," I replied.

"Can you use it in a sentence? Try to use it in a sentence.

I said, "Accept thine own self."

"Ah, I see. Who told you that?"

"If I told you, would you believe me?"

He got a serious look on his face and said, "Yes."

"God told me."

"What God?"

Getting upset, I pointed to the ceiling and said, "You know what God I'm talking about. The one up there." I thought he was playing games with me, so I said, "Never mind. That's all right."

"I'm sorry," he said. "I just had to know that you meant the same one."

"Yes, I did. Don't you know Him?"

He said, "Yes, I do know Him. Why did He say that to you?"

That made me nervous, but I said, "You know, like I told you, I'm different."

"Yes, but you didn't tell me *how* you're different."

I think he knew—but maybe not. Anyway, I said, "Well, I like girls."

"I like girls too," he said with a smile.

Wondering how to put it, finally I said, "I like girls the way I'm supposed to like boys." There, I'd finally said it.

"Why do you like them like that?" he asked.

"I don't know, but I always have."

"Who told you that you're supposed to like boys like that?"

"I don't know—the world, my family, everybody. You know, girls are supposed to like boys, and boys are supposed to like girls." I was getting upset again.

Then he said, "Well, maybe you just need a woman's type of love."

That was it! I'd found my answer. I *did* need a woman's type of love because I was different. I've always been different, and since then I've learned that different is okay. Everything and everybody is different in some way. As a child growing up, and even now as an adult, why did my difference have to be so hard to accept, so misunderstood, unnoticeable, and talked about? It was so hard for people to accept me, so hard to understand that God made me too, so easy not to notice that I'm human also, and so talked about without being acknowledged for who I am. Who cares? Anyway, I learned that God loves me and wants me to accept my own self ... and I did.

But before that, the chaplain said, "By the way, tell me how you and God happened to have this conversation."

What's a conversation? "I don't know that word either," I admitted.

"What did you and God talk about?"

Then I told him everything—how I wanted that beautiful woman, how I was afraid because men were there, and how I ran to pray in my unit. And finally, I told him how God spoke to me, saying, "My child, accept thine own self. I love you as you are ... My child, accept thine own self. I love you as you are ... My child, accept thine own self. I love you as you are."

The chaplain said, "That's all right. I just wanted to make sure that I was telling you the right thing."

He didn't have to say another word, because I had all the answers I needed—for then, that is. I thanked the chaplain, and he thanked me. Two answered prayers, I guess? That's when the chicken let the rooster out of the bag. In other words, I no longer cared who didn't like me or accept me. I knew that God loved me as I was, and I knew that I had to accept myself—and I did pretty good at it. For one thing, I got that pretty woman.

No, we didn't have sex in those years. Sex is not what I was seeking, unlike some people would assume. Later on, we did a little something-something, but don't worry. You won't get the nitty-gritty out of me, because then you'd start to judge me. And after all the dirty, low-down lust buckets that you fill up? Nope, you won't be judging me.

Hey, wait a minute. Don't get upset. I just might share something, like how I know that God loves and accepts homosexuals. Society has made *homosexual* a bad word, while cursing and profanity are accepted even on TV. Yeah, right, but who's zooming who? The word *zoo* is in *zooming*, ain't it? Well?

So you want to know what else happened between me and God, right? I don't think that a book could contain it. As I said, at that time I had my answer.

But other people and questions kept coming at me, and society even brainwashed me into feeling guilty. The nerve of it all, after I had heard from God! But temptations and trials do come to make you stronger, and *boy*—I mean, *girl*—did they come. Knock it off! Nothing personal, okay? Just because I said *boy* when I meant *girl*. Whatever! I wrote this book because I know that all kinds of people need to read it, okay? Well! That's what my sister would say: "Well!" If you were looking for an answer, she'd say, "Well …?" And if you got an answer, she'd still say, "Well …" Everything was *well*, and so it is. Well?

As I grew and became myself, people began to say that I was going to hell. They'd get upset, act out of character, and be downright ugly about me being gay. Gays at large, you know the deal? Preachers preached condemnation. This rooster was looking like a sitting duck for dinner. I had to go back to God because He and my chaplain friends were the only ones who seemed to understand.

I was out of prison by the time all this other stuff was going on. Everywhere I went, homosexuality was going to *helluality*. Oh yeah, I know what happened—I started going to church. I wanted to know more about

God, to be His friend and love Him back. But the way the churches put it, God didn't even want me in there. All I can say about that is who's zooming whom?

I still went to church and heard more about God, but it wasn't the same as Him speaking personally to me. I wanted the real deal because I needed to hear it, as they say, from the horse's mouth—and I did. No, I'm not calling God a horse, but He did use a donkey to speak, a hand to write, and a raven to feed a man named Elijah (Numbers 22:28–30, Daniel 5:5, and 1 Kings 17:6). Well?

I really couldn't read much, but one day I was locked down in another prison as punishment

(for something I didn't do), and a Bible was the only thing in the room to read. I said to God, "You must want me to read this book because there ain't nothing else to do in here."

I think He said, "Right."

Anyway, I said, "I don't know how to read, but if You teach me, I'll read it." I had fifty days to do in the hole, so I had time to read most all of it, and God taught me. I used to open the Bible and turn the pages, but when I would try to read it, the words just looked foreign to me. But I asked God to teach me to read so that I could know Him. I picked up that Bible one day and tried to read it, starting in the book of Matthew. But I just couldn't get it, because the word *begot* began to *beget* me. So I closed that Bible and said, "God, if You want me to read this, You've got to help me understand the words."

God said, "Turn to the beginning, the first page, and read." (He meant Genesis.) "'In the beginning ...' You know what that means, don't you? 'In the beginning' means in the beginning."

He was right. I knew that much, and so I began to read Genesis and found it interesting. I was understanding the words because God was teaching me to read. I was excited—and glad to be in the hole because I was with God and learning about Him.

God created the earth, His spirit was moving, He made light and people—everything! This was very understandable. Then I read His laws, history, and so on. It was just what I needed. I realized what God was doing for me while I was doing time for the devil. Well, I won't go there for the nonbelievers, but you'll soon find out. Anyway, I wanted to please God back, so I asked Him just to let me really know Him and be His friend, like other friends I knew.

God said to me, "I will favor you because you haven't asked for your freedom or for the warden [who I'd always ask for] or for phone calls or anything."

I said, "I'm for real, God. I want to know You because I like You. You're with me." Something like that. Anyway, right after that, God showed me in the Bible how Solomon asked God for an understanding heart (1 Kings 3:9–11). After reading that, I knew that God knew that I was for real. Ever since then, and even before that, He's been performing miracles for me. I knew then that God would always love me and care for me, and that's just what He does. He cares for me—and for you and you and you too. If you have multiple personalities, He cares for *all* of you. God knows what we need and meets us there. I needed Him, I needed to learn to read, I needed to like Him, to love Him ... and I still do.

Nope, this homosexual is not going to hell. Society's pressures and feelings of guilt from being gay would still sometimes upset and frighten me, but God helped me by showing me scriptures such as "What God hath cleansed, that call not thou common" (Acts 10:15), how we're no longer under the law (Galatians 3, 4:1–9), and many other scriptures of freedom. No matter what you might think, they've all worked for me. God removed my feelings of guilt and condemnation.

God even taught me about animals being homosexual so that I could know that He created relationships between them. For example, I wondered why I'm so much like a man, but then I read about the female bass fish. They have female babies, but after the babies turn five years old, many of them turn into males. I could relate to that. Then I found out that the male seahorse gives birth to his baby and almost dies in the process, and that gave me so much insight. I also learned that most male monkeys are homosexual and that many big white seagulls are lesbians. Some insects are both sexes, and on and on. Are they sinning? No, they just have relationships. This just shows how God is God of all. By the way, some of those homosexuals will probably enter heaven also.

But most people don't have all this knowledge, and my heart was still trying to condemn me. Then I read that even though our own hearts condemn us, God doesn't: "For if our heart condemns us, God is greater than our heart, and knoweth all things" (1 John 3:20). God is on my side, always here to give me the answers I need. God controls my mind and intervenes when I'm lost for truth. God allows me to face truth while constantly reminding me of His love and presence. He taught me His great secret, which is found in a question: "What is greater than you loving God?" The answer is God loving you! Some people might want to argue with me about how I need to put scripture in context, but I'll tell you that what works for me *is* for me.

Who can deny me God's greatness, His love for me, and His favor and mercy in my life? Nobody on the face of the earth can, and I dare you to try! God protects those whom He loves, even if He has to lift them up in midair. Even if He uses animals to teach us, His unlimited wisdom and miracles are beyond our ability to understand.

So don't get hung up on the burdens of life, which are usually other people. They're walking around and breathing just like us. Don't allow them to pull at your soul, for they are people without souls seeking to condemn you.

The worries and cares of this world will keep your eyes wet, your mind dumbfounded, and your entire being shaken and out of balance. Balance is so important, but we mainly hear of it in regard to material weight. Balance opens the eyes of the soul, where peace is offered and obtainable. Who could write such insight, wisdom, and truth? Yeah, that's right—a homosexual. Like God used the donkey that spoke and the writing on the wall and like the raven that fed Elijah. Also, one went up to heaven, while one, Saul, fell down from sin (2 Kings

2:11, Acts 9:1– 31). I can hardly contain these writings, which fill my body like the water and blood that it holds. Every sentence is a glimpse into the simple. Jesus Christ's appearance was so simple—it just was. Love is conceived in the heart, so simply. Why question it, when people are God's creations? Stay close to one another. Simple. You are needed, and needs manifest wants. I feel like John writing the book of Revelation. Eliphaz asked Job, "Art thou the first man that was born, or wast thou made before the hills?" (Job 15:7). In other words, who are you to judge anyone or know anything?

Let's go to Luke 17:34–36, which tells us that there will be two men in one bed, and one will be taken but the other will be left. The saved one will be taken? Yes, that's simple. Why were two men in one bed? That doesn't seem to be God's concern, but being saved is. Some translations of the Bible change those words, but doesn't the Bible tell us not to add to or take away His words? (See Revelation 22:18–19.) Well? *Well!* So don't go judging God's creations, whom He loves and adores. Woe unto you if you do! Someone has to give an account of what's real and true. The proof always lies in the lives of extraordinary people. You will not find them prejudiced, but understanding and humble.

Don't allow other people to tell you that you have to be anyone other than who you really are. That's trickery and lies. People with that kind of attitude are always looking for someone who is vulnerable. Those people aren't satisfied with life, and there's a hole within them that contains contagious contaminants. That is why so many people follow others, like the suicide crews. The leaders have the hole, and the crews, led by trickery, get contaminated. They forget that being themselves is just fine. Someone tells them that being different isn't good, so they all try to be the same. Nothing is ever the same except change, because change is change. Know that you are okay and that God loves you. Accept thine own self, and don't be contaminated by trickery and lies.

Now I shall free you and speak to your soul. Allow yourself to be filled with love and desires at ease. Why did you buy this book in the first place? You need it, but don't waste your time. You only understand it in the short run, but it goes on much longer, even forever.

Worry comes from complaints; stop complaining and your worries will cease. Do you know someone who always seems to be worried and uneasy, yet they are supposed to be righteous? Yeah, right. Well? You have your answer. Complaining? Sometimes one word is all you need. Stop! Complaining? Well? Society has taught us that a complete sentence must include a noun or pronoun and a verb. Well? *Well* does answer questions, so it's a complete sentence.

The Bible tells us that "the marriage bed is undefiled" (Hebrews 13:4). Yet some marriages aren't allowed, and most people who sleep in a bed together aren't married. Is anyone judging or bashing them? I didn't think so. Not like they judge and bash homosexual relationships. Why do you think God is allowing marriages to mix? You say it ain't God? Well, marriage is a blessing, and all blessings come from God. Yes, marriage is a blessing, although most people lose it, and why? Mostly because of other people from outside getting involved and creating misunderstandings. Am I lying? I don't think so. So do what you must and keep the outsiders out!

What about how someone dresses? The Bible tells us "whose adorning let it not be that outward adorning of plaiting the hair, and of wearing of gold, or of putting on of apparel; but let

it be the hidden man of the heart, in that which is not corruptible, even the ornament of a meek and quiet spirit, which is in the sight of God of great price" (1 Peter 3:3–4). Simple. What really counts, inside or out? Let your clothes count with your heart and dress it with love because love comes in many colors. Dress it with dignity because it pleases God above all others.

God's really all that matters because we come from and will return to Him, one way or another. Ask the people you know who are dead, for they do come back. If you don't believe me, just ask for a ghost. I dare you. Well? Then leave well enough alone. How do you dress? The answer should be warm in winter, cool in summer, and gay in spring. Well? Whatever! Damn, I like this book. Did I curse? Oh snap, well! How holy can one get? Real holey, like a raggedy pair of jeans. Think about it. Simple.

I could've named this book *Simple*, but of course no one would have bought it, get it? Simple. Light on, light off. Nothing hard about that, yet we argue about light switches too. When should the light be on? When needed, of course. This is really a problem in our society. Who knows? Who needs to know? Need knows! Get it? This is a heavy book (not in weight), but it will take effect in weight if we wait. There it goes again? Knowledge! Simply put! Ain't I (Bad) good? What's up, people? Stock market? No! Sky and rockets? Yeah! Oh well!

Take a bad person, for example, or someone with a negative attitude. (Is that you?) Learn from them, and learn not to be like them. To be or not to be is an answer, not a question. Didn't school mess you up? All that math about a dollar? All that history about what never happened? All that science about escaping reality? Someone wrote a book called *Lies My Teacher Told Me* Go figure! I think I'll buy the book and read it. Buy a book; buy a book; buy a book. Remember when we couldn't? Even you too. One day you couldn't. You could have been too young. See, people will just argue with you. That's one good thing about writing a book. You'll have one on them.

Society tells you who to marry. Marry a man or marry a woman, they say. I'm glad they know all the guarantees in life. While the world turns single, okay? I think I'll make up my own living, with God living within me. Get a taste of that for an answer. If needed, get your hole filled, life complete, no outsiders, only insiders … simple … complete.

I have got to get this book published! Have you ever said that, but then didn't? Shame, shame, shame. Do it. Feel it. Done!

Are you full yet? This is an all-you-can-eat book. Food is another thing that we enjoy, but they have a problem with that too. Problem, problem, solve them, solve them. Simple. Why so hard, so misunderstood, so unnoticeable, so talked about, so condemned? Well? Lacking! Don't complain about what they'll wear at your wedding. Just be thankful that they will or won't come. Now counting, count your blessings. Your day will not be boring, but full of grace. Continue to count your blessings, because if you don't, someone else will count them for you. Simple.

This book is so hot that I can hardly put it down. Yes, it's very hot, burning my soul with the warmth of love, caressing and embracing my way home to heaven. I bet a lot of you wanted to take "burning my soul" and run with it, right? But I'm too fast and too saved for you to run. Why do you think I wrote this book in the first place? First place!

Woe, it just comes naturally. Like the word *natural*, who possessed the animals to be homosexuals? Is *possessed* a good word or a bad word? It may not make much sense, but for sure you understand it. Stop running: the race is won (One). Common sense. Simple!

There is so much pressure in the world against being gay. Murder is more accepted. Isn't something wrong with this picture? All things are possible with God. If that's true, then why do we fear man? Was he here before the hills?

I wrote this book because God told me that in addition to being an artist, He would make me a writer. The purpose of this book is to help young people get on with their lives and not commit suicide. It's to encourage all people to come together because we're all accepted by God. These are simple words: whosoever; all things work together for good for those who love Him; for God so loved the world; love covers a multitude of sins; no longer condemned; for all have sinned; and in the beginning God created the heavens and the earth. These words can keep you in the right frame of mind for the rest of your life, and the *right* frame of mind is *your* mind.

Don't let other people tell you who you are or where you're going. They weren't here before the hills, and they don't know anything. They're only walking and breathing just like you are— walkers and breathers. You're just fine and you always were, even though someone told you different. When people try to judge you, say to them right out, "Well, just let me see you fly around awhile. Then come back and maybe we can talk." Well? Well! Leave people alone and get your own wings in shape. No one else can put them on for you, and you can't wear anyone else's.

I told you God told me to write this book. Do you think I could write such insight? No! Only by His might. I already told you how I feel about science. Here's my philosophy about people: "Some do, some don't. Some will, some won't. Some people like coffee, some people like tea, some people like both, and some people like neither."

So what're you gonna do? Back off, before you get smacked off by the big man who's got my back! Sorry, I had to get that off. When you write a book, no one can argue with you, so I'll say this: "Nah, nah, nah, nah, nah!" Now I was joking, but seriously joking.

My goal is to get out a powerfully effective message about love. True life is about love, harmony, and living. Otherwise you just exist, like a rock that's just occupying space. And just like a stone, eventually you'll be blasted away. You can bank on that.

Establish a new dictionary of words that are alive and moving. (Yeah, I'm doing that.) People will try to hinder you from being who you are. I like me—and I do, I do, I do love me. Say "I

do" to yourself before you say "I do" to someone else, and then really do for yourself what the words *I do* are supposed to mean. Some people say talk is cheap, but I say talk is words and somebody is going to understand them. Don't allow "no one" when God said "whosoever."

Some of you are really getting it. Think about trees that look withered, old, and dead. Before you judge them, wait until their season has come upon them, and then ask yourself, *Did I create these?* Who are you to judge? You are made only of dust, and you will return to dust. If you don't believe, visit a graveyard. Just think about it. Why aren't you only loving, and loving only people? That's the maximum love you can render to God because God loves people more than anything. When you judge someone, you are missing your opportunity to receive peace and love. Hey, I can't say it any better. If you don't get that, you'd better ask somebody. You say, "I don't judge, but the Bible says …" Yeah, right. Does the Bible say to judge your brother or sista? Did it say to ratify your judgment? If people feel the need to judge someone else, there must be a good thing going on, because when it comes to really doing a good thing, ain't nobody heard

nothing! Am I lying or what?

A spirit does rise and live again. Have you ever had an experience that seemed familiar, like maybe it happened before, like déjà vu? Your spirit travels faster than your physical body does. Have you ever had a dream in which you were flying? Have you ever been running, crying in your dream, yet your physical body is asleep?

God uses who He chooses, and I'm the one who's helping you now. Don't judge me, because you're not wise, compassionate, or righteous enough to do that. You don't have, nor can you obtain, the credentials to do that. If someone peeped in on every hour of your day, you'd be caught doing something not so righteous. If someone looked at everything that you've ever possessed, even all that you gave away, your unrighteousness would be exposed. Everyone reading this book, and even myself—the Bible tells us that all have sinned.

Yet this book is about sorrow, not sin. Where there's sorrow, there's change, and change is good. It's sorrow when you criticize a person, and you'll have to suffer and be sorry for that, but your suffering will make you change. The more you suffer, the more you change. The less you suffer, the more you adjust.

God took David, a shepherd boy, and made him a king. David had no friends, but God used people who were considered lowlife to be David's loyal friends. The Bible records that David had about four hundred friends. How many loyal friends do you have? Who can you trust? I bet you could count them on one hand and still have fingers left over. If you don't know, you'd better ask somebody.

Be in love. With who? Be in love with the life that God gives each of us. Life is full and never dull. Count your blessings, and that will get you through your days. Do things you enjoy. What do you enjoy? How many things do you enjoy? How many things are there? Simple. You know

God really loves us, so learn to love Him back. That takes a lot of time. You must love everyone, and what if everyone loved you?

Don't worry about other people. Remember, they're just walkers and breathers. You know people will tell you wrong things. For example, if your favorite color is yellow, like mine is, they might say, "No, yellow can't be your favorite color, because ..." Whatever. How can anyone else tell you what you like? If people had all the answers, they wouldn't be people. Yet scientists think they really know living. Living is life, and life just simply is. It's too broad to hold but narrow enough to behold.

Who can speak the language of God unless God giveth? Who can God use? Who does God use? I'm the same one who ... Aren't you the same one who ...? Who will give you your last meal? Will it be a stranger?

Yet the world teaches us not to talk to strangers. Who's a stranger? Be fearless, and you won't know a stranger. How can you be fearless? Fear God most!

Misunderstandings occur often in relationships, followed by pain, misspoken words, and even violence. All for what? Release. People lash out and try to grab, stab, shoot, and drown, just to get rid of the hurt. But hurt cannot be grabbed, stabbed, shot, or drowned. It must be dealt with, accepted, and allowed to go through you. Pain cuts like a knife and tears your heart open, making room for more pain. But over time you'll heal, and then you'll have more smiles and happiness to share. Then more pain. It's life.

Heaven is supposed to be a place where there is no more pain, but down here pain comes in many forms. That's why prayer is so important. Someone needs to stay strong and positive and keep hope alive. Otherwise everyone suffers longer.

Accept the hurt like surgery, take the medicine of prayer three times a day, watch over the hurt, make sure no dirt gets in it, and move slowly until you can stand tall again. Be of use as you can, drink plenty of water, make yourself do it, go to the bathroom, sing a little, hum a little, and don't ever forget to smile. Someone will be there with a card, flowers, a prayer, and a care, for you do not hurt alone and you are not alone.

Misunderstandings can go a long way, as far as the ends of the earth. If you're part of a misunderstanding that goes that far, imagine rolling a bowling ball and trying to make a strike. If you miss, don't worry, because at least the ball has been rolled. Put pain, hurt, suffering, and pressure down at the end of that bowling lane, and roll another ball. Keep rolling until you see things clear. Put people on the track too. Oh well!

Life isn't easy. I won't tell that lie. It took God six days to create the world, and He's God. We must learn to wait better and more regularly. It's okay to wait. We wait to use the bathroom or bake a cake, we wait for payday, we wait to eat and sleep, and we wait for people and things. Wait on God!

Ask Him to intervene and help you overcome heartache, pain, and even the pain of other

people misjudging you. Do you ever get accused of being a villain? Most honorable people do, but remember that those are the people chosen by God. He knows you have courage and bravery. He knows your heart is good and that you try to do things for the greater good, for yourselves and others.

Maybe you're a villain, and maybe you became that way because you were violated. Many people have been violated. God cares a great deal about people to whom wrong is done, and people who inflict pain and do wrong have yet to suffer even more. Woe unto them!

This book might confuse you a bit, so read it two or three times. Each time you'll be fed more as its simplicity unfolds. You'll feel like a flower that's about to open and reveal its beauty. That's all there is to it—beauty. That's God's plan for the world and the hereafter. That's what heaven is all about, and I'm going there. By the way, which homosexuals will go to heaven? All the saved ones! Are you saved? Well, I'll see you when I see you. Peace out!

Relationships

Brenda A. Dudley

Any Thoughts, Write Them Here

Someone Cares

Brenda A. Dudley

Brenda A. Dudley was born in Washington, DC, in 1956, and her mother had eleven children; Brenda is a left-handed middle child, and her initials spell BAD, which became her childhood nickname. Brenda lived a wayward life on the streets of DC, skipping school and following the wrong crowd, which landed her in jail. Although she spent most of her youth incarcerated, she was able to accept Jesus Christ as her Lord and Savior. Today she has received many miracles, like earning her GED and two college degrees, and she has overcome bad habits like substance abuse and criminal activities. Brenda is a cancer survivor and has experienced many hardships, but she can always give someone an ear, a smile, and a word or sight of encouragement.

www.ingramcontent.com/pod-product-compliance
Lightning Source LLC
La Vergne TN
LVHW041548060526
838200LV00037B/1197